MR. TOPSY-TURVY

by Roger Hargreaves

D0192803

Mr Topsy Turvy was a funny sort of a fellow.

Everything about him was either upside down, or inside out, or back to front – topsy turvy in fact.

It was all very extraordinary!

To give you some idea of how topsy turvy Mr Topsy Turvy was, you ought to see his house.

The front door is upside down to start with.

And the curtains hang upside down at the windows.

And just look at that chimney pot!

All very extraordinary!

Inside is the same.

Just look at the clock standing on Mr Topsy Turvy's mantelpiece.

Isn't that the topsiest turviest clock you've ever seen?

And just look at the way Mr Topsy Turvy reads a book.

Not only does he read it upside down, but he starts to read it at the back page!

And just look where Mr Topsy Turvy puts the stamp when he sends a letter to somebody.

Have you ever seen anything like it?

Mr Smith
High Street
the Town

Now, this story is all about the time Mr Topsy Turvy came to the town where you and I live.

Nobody is quite sure how Mr Topsy Turvy got there, or where he came from, but he did arrive, because somebody saw him getting off the train.

The trouble was, he did it in a topsy turvy way, and got out the wrong side and fell on to the railway line.

Which really isn't all that surprising, is it?

When he'd picked himself up and managed to find his way out of the station, Mr Topsy Turvy went to a hotel to find a room to spend the night.

The hotel manager tried not to smile when he saw Mr Topsy Turvy walk into his hotel carrying his suitcase upside down and with his topsy turvy hat on his head.

"Good afternoon, sir," he said. "Can I help you?"

Now, something you didn't know about Mr Topsy Turvy is the way he speaks.

You see, he sometimes gets things the wrong way round.

"Afternoon good," said Mr Topsy Turvy to the hotel manager. "I'd room a like!"

The manager scratched his head. "You mean you'd like a room?" he asked.

"Please yes," replied Mr Topsy Turvy.

Eventually the hotel manager managed to work out what Mr Topsy Turvy was talking about, and he was taken up in the lift to a bedroom.

Then Mr Topsy Turvy unpacked his suitcase, put on his pyjamas, and went to bed.

He was rather tired after travelling from wherever he'd come from.

The following day Mr Topsy Turvy went round the town.

But what a fuss his going round the town caused.

He took a taxi from the hotel, but so confused the taxi driver trying to tell him where he wanted to go, the poor man drove straight into a traffic light.

"Oh dear," said Mr Topsy Turvy. "I am sorry very!"

Then he went into a big department store in the middle of the town.

He walked up to one of the counters.

"I'd like a sock of pairs," he said to the lady behind the counter.

"You mean a pair of socks," she smiled, and showed him a pair of bright red socks.

Mr Tospy Turvy put them on his hands!

Then he tried to leave, but being Mr Topsy Turvy he tried to walk down the up escalator, and all the people who were going up the up escalator all fell over themselves.

It was a terrible topsy turvy jumble!

That day Mr Topsy Turvy did all sorts of topsy turvy things.

He walked backwards across a street crossing, and caused an enormous traffic jam.

He went to a library and put all the books upside down on the shelves, and made everybody extremely cross.

Then he went to an art gallery and insisted on hanging all the pictures upside down so that he could look at them properly.

And then, after Mr Topsy Turvy had been in the town for just one day, he disappeared.

Nobody knew how he went, or where he went, but he certainly went because he wasn't there any more.

The whole town breathed a sigh of relief.

But . . .

What the town discovered, even though Mr Topsy Turvy had left, was that everything was still topsy turvy.

"Read all it about," shouted the newspaper sellers, instead of shouting, "Read all about it".

"News is the here," said the television newsreader, instead of saying, "Here is the news".

"Morning good," people started saying to each other when they met, and "Do do you how?" instead of, "How do you do?"

Everybody was talking topsy turvy!

Can you think of something to say that's topsy turvy?

Go on, try!

Fantastic offers for Mr. Men fans!

Collect all your Mr. Men or Little Miss books in these superb durable collectors' cases!

Only £5.99 inc. postage and packing, these wipe-clean, hard-wearing cases will give all your Mr. Men or Little Miss books a beautiful new home!

Keep track of your collection with this giant-sized double-sided Mr. Men and Little Miss Collectors' poster.

Collect 6 tokens and we will send you a brilliant giant-sized double-sided collectors' poster! Simply tape a £1 coin to cover postage and packaging in the space provided and fill out the form overleaf.

Only need a few Mr. Men or Little Miss to complete your set? You can order any of the titles on the back of the books from our Mr. Men order line on 0870 787 1724. Orders should be delivered between 5 and 7 working days.

--- **TO BE COMPLETED BY AN ADULT** ---

To apply for any of these great offers, ask an adult to complete the details below and send this whole page with the appropriate payment and tokens, to: MR. MEN CLASSIC OFFER, PO BOX 715, HORSHAM RH12 5WG

☐ Please send me a giant-sized double-sided collectors' poster.
AND ☐ I enclose 6 tokens and have taped a £1 coin to the other side of this page.

☐ Please send me ☐ Mr. Men Library case(s) and/or ☐ Little Miss library case(s) at £5.99 each inc P&P

☐ I enclose a cheque/postal order payable to Egmont UK Limited for £.....................

OR ☐ Please debit my MasterCard / Visa / Maestro / Delta account (delete as appropriate) for £.....................

Card no. ☐☐☐☐☐☐☐☐☐☐☐☐☐☐☐☐☐☐☐   Security code ☐☐☐

Issue no. (if available) ☐   Start Date ☐☐/☐☐/☐☐   Expiry Date ☐☐/☐☐/☐☐

Fan's name: ....   Date of birth: ....

Address: ....

....

....   Postcode: ....

Name of parent / guardian: ....

Email for parent / guardian: ....

Signature of parent / guardian: ....

Please allow 28 days for delivery. Offer is only available while stocks last. We reserve the right to change the terms of this offer at any time and we offer a 14 day money back guarantee. This does not affect your statutory rights. Offers apply to UK only.

☐ We may occasionally wish to send you information about other Egmont children's books.
If you would rather we didn't, please tick this box.

Ref: MRM 001